Also by Sheryl Berk and Carrie Berk

The Cupcake Club Series
Peace, Love, and Cupcakes

Recipe for Trouble

Winner Bakes All

Icing on the Cake

Baby Cakes

Royal Icing

Sugar and Spice

Sweet Victory

Fashion Academy Series
Fashion Academy

FASHION
ACADEMY

Runway
Ready

Sheryl Berk & Carrie Berk

sourcebooks
jabberwocky

Published by Sourcebooks Jabberwocky, an imprint of Sourcebooks, Inc.
P.O. Box 4410, Naperville, Illinois 60567-4410
(630) 961-3900
Fax: (630) 961-2168
www.sourcebooks.com

Library of Congress Cataloging-in-Publication data is on file with the publisher.

Source of Production: Versa Press, East Peoria, Illinois, USA
Date of Production: November 2015
Run Number: 5005220

Printed and bound in the United States of America.
VP 10 9 8 7 6 5 4 3 2 1

To Uncle Charles—You've patiently waited for a book

to be dedicated to you! You rock!

Designer Dreams

Mackenzie "Mickey" Williams was having a dream—her favorite one. In it, she was showing her very first collection under the tents at Lincoln Center during New York Fashion Week. The lights flashed and the music pulsed as supermodels strutted down the runway dressed in her elaborate, colorful designs. There was Gigi Hadid, wearing a black-velvet strapless jumpsuit and gold fringed poncho! There was Kendall

Jenner, posing in a sapphire-blue pleather romper! There was Karlie Kloss, looking fierce in a red neoprene minidress and matching scuba jacket!

As each look appeared onstage, the crowd of celebrities and fashion magazine editors oohed and aahed and applauded enthusiastically. At the end of the show, Mickey walked down the runway and bowed dramatically as the crowd leaped to their feet and cheered.

Backstage, Mickey was suddenly mobbed by models, fans, and press, all eager to tell her how much they loved her collection. They handed her bouquets of roses, so many she couldn't hold them all in her arms.

"Mickey, darling, you have outdone yourself!" gushed *Vogue* editor Anna Wintour. "What a stellar debut!"

"Aww, it was nothing," Mickey replied in her dream.

"Oh, but it is!" Legendary designer Karl Lagerfeld reached over to shake her hand. He was wearing his sunglasses as always, and his snowy white hair was pulled back in a ponytail. "It's divine."

"Oh, Karl, that means so much to me coming from you!" Mickey exclaimed. "You're one of my idols."

"*Who's Karl?*" A high-pitched, nasal voice shattered the beautiful moment. "Mackenzie, do you know it's seven forty-five? You're going to miss the school bus."

Mickey bolted up in bed. "Aunt Olive, I was talking to Karl Lagerfeld!" She moaned, stretching her hands over her head. "You know, the head designer for the House of Chanel? It was the best dream ever."

Her aunt handed her a glass of green sludge. "Have your kale shake. It'll wake you right up."

"I don't wanna wake up." Mickey groaned. "I want to go back to my dream. I wish it was true."

Olive patted her on the arm. "Well, if you keep wowing them at that fashion school of yours, it'll happen one day. But not if you're late!"

Mickey made the bus with only seconds to spare. She settled into a seat and rested her head against the cold glass window, watching as the city streets whizzed by. Her first day at the Fashion Academy of Brooklyn—a.k.a. FAB—seemed like a lifetime ago. But it had been just five months since she left her mom and best friend, Annabelle, in Philly and moved in with Aunt Olive in NYC so she could attend *the* middle school for budding fashion designers.

It wasn't easy. Besides Mickey missing her mom and friend terribly, in the beginning, nobody at

FAB quite "got" her fashion sense. She thought it was perfectly acceptable to mix clashing patterns, sew lace on a leather motorcycle jacket, wear two different-colored shoes, or streak her hair with colored chalk. It was exciting and innovative, and if there was one thing Mickey loved, it was thinking outside the box.

Ever since she was a little girl, she had created one-of-a-kind outfits for her dolls and, later, for herself. For five dollars at the flea market, she could find a sad, abandoned old dress, riddled with stains or holes, and transform it into something chic, sleek, and unique. She felt like a fashion superhero with magical powers!

According to Mickey, fashion was all about forging your own vision and not letting anyone dictate your personal style. "Whatever you wear," she'd instructed her friend Annabelle over winter break, "you should make it your own."

"Bella Thorne says pastel is in for spring," Annabelle had pointed out, waving a *Teen Vogue* in Mickey's face.

"Boring...and predictable," Mickey said, glancing at the photo of the fashionista in a buttercup-yellow sweater and white jeans. "I'd cut that sweater into a crop top and pair it with something graphic—like an ikat-print wrap skirt."

Annabelle looked confused. "What's an ikat? Is that like an iPad?"

Mickey giggled. When it came to fashion lingo, Anna was kind of clueless. "It's a dyeing technique used to pattern textiles," she explained to her friend.

Annabelle shook her head. "I still don't get it. But I'm sure if you designed for Bella, she'd look amazing."

If only! Mickey desperately wanted to have her own fashion label one day, one that stars begged to wear on the red carpet. It was the reason she'd jumped at the chance to attend FAB, even if her mom hadn't been enthusiastic about the idea.

"You're eleven," her mother had protested when the acceptance letter came. "I don't know how I feel about you living in New York City."

"It's not like I'll be living on Jupiter," Mickey had pointed out. "It's just a train ride away and I'll come home every weekend. Besides, I'll be staying with Aunt Olive."

Her mom's sister wasn't an easy egg to crack, but Mickey had won her over—and even helped her come out of her shell. Aunt Olive had recently traded in her severe business suits and sensible shoes for a purple wool trapeze jacket and leather boots.

"You like it?" she'd asked Mickey as she modeled it in their living room.

"It's so cool." Mickey applauded her. "The color is very bold and regal, and those boots are fierce."

"Is that good?" Olive asked, scratching her head. "Do I want to be fierce?"

"You do!" Mickey chuckled. "Especially in the workplace. You want to show your bosses you're not afraid of hard work. You can handle anything."

"And my clothes say that?"

"They speak volumes," Mickey assured her. "That's what's so incredible about fashion. It can talk for you and about you."

"Well, then," Olive said, checking her look one more time in the mirror. "My look is saying, 'Olive, better get a move on! You've got a legal brief due in less than an hour!'"

The students at FAB were a whole other story. When an assignment called for an original design for a World Hunger T-shirt, of course Mickey decided to adorn hers with real food. The only problem was that it spoiled overnight.

"They think I'm a freak," she had complained during her first weeks to her one confidant, JC. He knew a thing or two about how to navigate the social scene at FAB. He was a year older and a seventh-grader, not to mention a brilliant designer of canine couture.

"Well, you do smell like cabbage," he pointed out. "And your hair looks like you dipped it in creamed spinach."

"I thought everyone at FAB would be creative and edgy," Mickey said with a sigh. "I've always had my own sense of style. I thought here it would be welcome."

JC nodded. "I get it. You like to stand out. But this"—he pointed to her neon-yellow combat boots and green-plaid leggings with ripped knees—"this might be taking it a bit too far. Unless you're Lady Gaga, that is."

He gave her an extreme makeover so that the kids at FAB wouldn't be so distracted by her outward appearance that they couldn't appreciate her talent.

He instructed her to wash the green highlights out of her hair, then gave her a new name (Kenzie Wills), a new identity (daughter of a famous Finnish designer), and a streamlined new look. "Less is more," he taught her. "No more hair chalk highlights. Lose the neon sneakers and ditch the crazy hats."

As Kenzie, Mickey's popularity soared. Even Jade Lee, the school's reigning queen bce, was curious. Mickey loved the attention and the acceptance, but hated pretending to be someone she wasn't. When she was chosen as a finalist for FAB's first-semester Runway Showdown, her mission was clear: "I gotta be me!" Her Cinderella-inspired ball gown with a rainbow tulle under-layer stopped the show.

So here she was at the start of her second semester, back to being just Mickey. Thanks to the Showdown, she'd finally earned respect for her designs—even if she did come in second place to Jade.

Jade held court in the FAB hallway every morning. Mickey had to admit that the girl was chic. Today, she wore a petal-pink, long-sleeved DVF wrap dress and knee-high suede boots, and her long, shiny black hair was swept back into a rhinestone headband. She could have easily stepped out of the pages of a magazine—a walking, talking mannequin! Did she ever have a bad hair day? Were her clothes ever wrinkled?

Her twin brother, Jake, was equally dapper. Mickey noted his red Ralph Lauren cashmere sweater and the black Prada messenger bag slung over his shoulder. Of course, it didn't hurt that their mother was Bridget Lee, designer to Hollywood's biggest stars. Thanks to Mommy, the duo not only got to wear any designer duds their hearts desired, but also had unlimited access to the red carpet and got to rub elbows with celebrities. When she was watching *Extra* with Aunt Olive, Mickey was sure she had spotted Jade looming behind Jennifer Lawrence at an NYC movie. Of course she was! Her mom had designed JLaw's stunning silver lamé gown.

Jade shot Mickey a dirty look as she passed by. "You know what they say about second place," she said loudly so Mickey wouldn't miss a word. "It's the first one to lose." Though several weeks and winter break has passed since that day, Jade was never going to let Mickey live down the fact that she'd lost to her at the Runway Showdown.

Let her gloat, Mickey thought to herself. *Winning isn't everything.* She had learned a lot about herself in creating that collection and was even featured on a famous fashion blogger's site. So what if Jade beat her? There would be many more fashion challenges and chances to show Jade—and all of FAB—that she was a fashion force to be reckoned with.

"Don't pay any attention to her." Mickey's classmate South East ran to catch up with her.

"She's just sore that your collection rocked." At least South was on her side!

"So," her friend continued, "do I call you Mickey or Kenzie? I think it's cool you have two names. You know musicians change theirs all the time—like Diddy was once Puff Daddy, P. Diddy, and before that Sean Combs."

Mickey nodded. "I'm just Mickey. Kenzie Wills will be the name of my design house."

"Cool," South replied, then quickly changed the subject. "Did you have a great winter break? I did! My dad took me to Hollywood where he's recording his new album. We hung out with J. T. and Pharrell—"

Mickey cut her off. She knew if she didn't, South would chew her ear off with endless stories of her fabulous rap-star dad Laser East. Mickey was anxious to get to class and see what Mr. Kaye had up his sleeve today for them to design.

"Yeah, break was fun. Lots of time back home in Philly with the family. Gotta go!" she said. "See you in Apparel Arts!"

Mission Impossible

Mr. Kaye was quite the master at inventing original—and perplexing—fashion design challenges for his students. Mickey had come to accept that she would never know what to expect when he walked through the studio door and drew a number on the SMART Board.

"So you've all survived my previous challenges," he said, counting them off on his fingertips. "There was the World Hunger shirt, then 'Everything Old Is New Again,' then 'ABC Inspiration'…"

"And don't forget 'Fairy-Tale Makeover,'" Gabriel reminded him. "My Red Riding Hood red leather miniskirt was *sick*."

Mr. Kaye frowned. He hated when students didn't raise their hands.

"Yes, yes, I was getting to that one," their teacher said. "And for the record, I prefer *chic* to *sick*." He sniffed.

Gabriel sunk lower in his seat. "I guess that's why he gave me a two on it," he whispered to Mickey. Mr. Kaye's grading scale was simple:

four was FABulous; three, decent; two, disappointing; one, a fashion failure.

Mr. Kaye clapped his hands together to silence the chatter. "All of those previous challenges pale in comparison to this one. And of course, as always, the students with the highest total grades on the semester's assignments get to compete in the final Runway Showdown. So make this one count!"

Mickey's classmate Mars (really Marceline) was seated next to her and groaned loudly. "We're in for it."

Mr. Kaye pulled a sewing kit out of his desk. "Do you see this?" he asked, waving it in the air. "For this challenge, you can't use any of the items inside."

"What?" Mars gasped. "No needle? No thread? No way!"

"Yes, way!" Mr. Kaye insisted. "I call this challenge 'Oh No! No Sew.' The look you create must be constructed entirely without sewing, either by hand or by machine."

"That's crazy," South said, bursting into the room. "How are we supposed to make the pieces of our pattern stick together?"

Mr. Kaye shrugged. "Alas, that is not my problem—it's yours. As is the tardy you will receive for coming late to class today."

South took her seat and opened her notebook to jot down instructions.

"What about staples? Glue stick?" Mickey asked.

"Bubble gum?" Gabriel piped up.

"All options, should you choose them," Mr. Kaye replied. "The decision is yours." He gave them the remainder of the class to sketch, but Mickey couldn't come up with a single idea.

"A blank page after twenty minutes? That's not like you, Mickey," Mr. Kaye said, peering over her shoulder. "I thought you thrived on creativity."

"I do," Mickey said. "I can think of a million outfits I'd like to make, but they all need to be stitched together."

"Think harder," Mr. Kaye said. "I'm sure you'll come up with something that speaks to our challenge."

Stormy Weather

Mickey was actually grateful for a rainy week-end back at home in Philly. Her mom had to work all day at Wanamaker's Department Store, and it was too cold and damp to venture outside. So Mickey sat in her room, munching on microwave popcorn and trying to come up with something—anything—that would earn her a four on Mr. Kaye's latest design challenge.

She called her friend Annabelle for advice.

"You're asking me?" her BFF said. "Mickey, I can't sew a button on."

"Exactly!" Mickey insisted. "That's why you're the perfect person to help me with my homework. No sewing allowed."

"Hmmm," Annabelle said. "Have you thought about origami? You could maybe fold a cool jacket out of a giant sheet of paper."

Mickey chewed on her pencil eraser. "It's not a bad idea, but I'm not really sure I could find a piece of paper that was big enough."

"Tape a bunch of sheets together," Annabelle suggested. "Tape is okay, right?"

Mickey dug in her desk drawer and pulled out

a pack of colored construction paper and a roll of Scotch tape. "I guess I could give it a shot. Thanks!"

Two hours later, she had taped thirty sheets together and managed to fold a giant paper airplane but no stylish jacket, shirt, or skirt. Her fingers were covered with Band-Aids from all the paper cuts. She'd wasted the entire day trying to make a design work and still had nothing to show for it.

"Ugh!" she said, tossing the mess of folded paper in the corner of her room. "I give up!"

"Mickey Mouse! I'm home!" her mom called from the front door. "And I brought Chinese takeout with me." Mickey's mother, Jordana, dropped her umbrella on the floor and stood there in a plastic rain poncho, making a giant puddle on the floor.

"It's a hurricane out there," she said as Mickey took the bag of food from her. "I had to buy this ugly rain poncho at Wanamaker's so I wouldn't drown on the walk home."

Mickey giggled. Her mom looked like she had draped herself in plastic wrap. The hood hung in her eyes and the sleeves were so long that they covered her hands and dangled to her knees.

"Make fun of me all you want," Jordana said, peeling off her wet clothes. "At least it kept me dry in the storm. I'm sure you could whip up something a lot more fashionable, but it did the trick."

Mickey suddenly stopped laughing and snatched the soggy poncho off the floor. "That's it."

"What's it?" her mom asked.

"You just gave me an idea for my Apparel Arts assignment. What's a piece of clothing that you can wear that has no seams or stitches?"

Her mother flopped down on the couch and put her tired, aching feet up on the coffee table. "Is this a riddle?"

"No, it's a solution. One I've been searching for all day."

Her mother closed her eyes and rested her head on the couch pillows. "That's great, honey. Maybe you can go work on it and let me catch a quick nap before dinner."

Mickey was already down the hall in her room, rummaging through the scraps of leftover fabric she kept in her closet. There weren't many large pieces left, but she found some white linen that had been too scratchy to use on a dress. She rolled it out on the floor so she could take a few quick measurements.

"That should do it," she said aloud as she used her pencil to draw three circles on the material— one in the center and two on either side—before snipping away with her scissors. Then she dug in her drawer and found a large box of safety pins. She pinned one on the fabric and breathed a sigh of relief. It wasn't the best design she'd ever made, but it would do just fine.

Mickey always looked forward to second-period Apparel Arts class, but today she was nervous. She wasn't sure that her design was "up to snuff" as Mr. Kaye liked to say. It felt a bit simple, but what was she supposed to do? Telling her she couldn't sew was like tying her hands behind her back. To make anything halfway decent, she needed more time, more material, more safety pins…

She was so busy fretting over her design that she didn't notice Ms. Ratzner staring straight at her in Fashion History class. "Mickey Williams, can you tell the class who invented blue jeans in the eighteen sixties?"

"Huh? What?" Mickey said, snapping out of her trance as she heard her name called.

"I asked you for the name of the person who invented blue jeans."

Mickey hemmed and hawed. She had forgotten to do the class reading over the weekend. "Mr. Gap?" she finally guessed. The class roared with laughter.

"Levi Strauss," Ms. Ratzner replied, annoyed. "Did you do your homework?"

Mickey shook her head. "I'm sorry. It must have slipped my mind. I was so busy with my Apparel Arts assignment."

"No excuse," her teacher replied, making a note in her grade book. "If you want to be a successful designer in the future, you need to understand the fashion of the past. It's our foundation."

Mickey nodded. She knew her teacher was right. "I'm sorry. It won't happen again."

"No," Ms. Ratzner said firmly. "It won't. If you want to remain at FAB, you must pass all of your classes—not just Mr. Kaye's."

Mickey was still smarting from Ms. Ratzner's scolding when she got to Apparel Arts the next period. No one else looked worried; in fact, they all seemed proud and happy with their designs. Gabriel was cheerfully putting his work on the dress form next to his desk.

"What is that material?" Mars asked, circling around the shiny, black cropped jacket.

"It's electrical tape," he replied. "Cool, huh? I found a ton of it in my dad's toolbox. No sewing, just sticking."

"How do you like my design?" South entered

the room modeling a red-and-yellow woven maxi skirt.

"It looks like a pot holder I made my mom in second grade." Gabriel snickered.

"That's *exactly* what it is," South said. "I used those stretchy little loops and a loom to make it. But no sewing!"

"Very cool," Gabriel said. "I never would have thought of that."

"Mine is even more genius," Mars said, unzipping her garment bag. She pulled out a tube top she'd fashioned by cutting the top off a red beanie hat. She hot-glued on silver sequins and made a belt entirely from shiny silver soda-can tops. "I just tied them together with dental floss."

Mickey gulped. Everyone's work was amazing—so much more amazing than hers.

"So, what did you do?" South asked her. "I bet it's something really over the top."

"Well, it's over the head…" Mickey said, pulling the poncho out of her bag. She'd used the safety pins to make a crisscross pattern along the bottom edges.

Her classmates were speechless—until Gabriel broke the silence. "It looks like a giant diaper."

Mickey took a step back and tried to look at her design objectively. "OMG, you're totally right. It *does* look like a giant diaper!"

But it was too late to make any changes. Mr. Kaye walked in and sat on the edge of his desk. "Class, I can't wait to see what you've come up with for me today."

Everyone presented, and Mr. Kaye took notes and gave constructive criticism. "I think you could have pushed the envelope more," he told Mars. "A belt is fine. But what more could have been done with the can tops? A vest? An entire coat? Open your mind to the possibilities."

Mars nodded. "I made my brother drink two six packs of soda this weekend so I could have the tops," she said. "A coat might take a year!"

When he came to Gabriel's jacket, Mr. Kaye

stopped and stared. "Gabriel, the workmanship is flawless. Using tape instead of material was a big risk, but it paid off. I'm wowed."

Gabriel beamed and elbowed Mickey. "Totally rocked it."

Finally, it was Mickey's turn. Mr. Kaye paused at her dress form and wrinkled his brow. "I'm confused," he said slowly. "What were you going for?"

"A poncho," Mickey said meekly. "With a safety pin pattern on the bottom."

"I fear it misses the mark," Mr. Kaye said. "It feels uninspired to me."

Mickey could feel the tears welling in the corners of her eyes. "I tried. Really. I thought it was okay…but I guess I just gave up and made something to get it over with."

Mr. Kaye faced the class. "Let this be a lesson to all of you," he said. "All designers have their bad days, even their bad collections. We learn from our mistakes. We become better designers because of them."

Mickey saw him write the number two in his grade book next to her name. She knew that meant Mr. Kaye was disappointed in her—and worse, she was disappointed in herself.

A New Challenge

Mickey made herself a promise that she would never again present something that she didn't one hundred percent love. Her heart had to be in the design as much as her handiwork. Still, the challenge had rattled her confidence.

"You'll get over it," JC assured her at lunch that same day. "I got a two on a tie assignment Mr. Kaye gave us last year. I designed mine with lots of little dog bones all over it, and he hated it. He said it was for the dogs—which it was. But our client wasn't canine—he was a Wall Street executive."

Mickey shrugged. "But you did better on the next one?"

"Yeserooni," JC said. "Not doing well on the tie assignment was a great kick in the butt. It made me work harder, and I created one of my finest fashion masterpieces." He pulled his phone out of his pocket and showed her a picture of a stunning turquoise-blue jumpsuit with white suede fringe around the plunging neckline. "We had to be inspired by a holiday gift—something we gave or received. I chose to be inspired by the box it came in: a Tiffany blue box with a white ribbon."

Mickey zoomed in on the details. "It's breath-taking. Really."

"And it earned me a four. Not a bad way to bounce back, huh?"

Mickey tried to remember what JC had said and convince herself she would bounce back too. She usually came to Apparel Arts class eager and excited. But today, just one day after the diaper fiasco, she felt defeated and insecure.

"Chin up, Mickey," Mr. Kaye said, noticing how sad she looked. "I have a good feeling that you will redeem yourself on my next challenge."

Mickey sat up straight in her chair. "You do? What is it?"

"I call it, 'Grandma's Favorite Munchkin,'" he replied.

Gabriel raised his hand. "As in *The Wizard of Oz*? Are we designing Dorothy a new look? Retooling Glinda's gown into something a little less pink and poofy?"

Mr. Kaye pushed his spectacles to the tip of his nose and glared. "No, I am using the word 'munchkin' to refer to someone rather small and adorable."

"If he makes us design an outfit for a hamster, I am *not* going to be happy," Mars whispered to Mickey.

Mr. Kaye continued. "Clients can be extremely difficult," he said. "And part of becoming a successful designer is learning how to interpret what they want and give it to them."

Mickey gulped. What if the client was the same Wall Street exec that had earned JC his two last year?

Instead, a little girl strolled into the room and stood facing the students. She was dressed in a pink-and-white smocked dress, white ruffled socks, and shiny black Mary Janes.

"Aww, she's so cute!" Mars cooed. "Hiya, sweetie!"

The child stuck her tongue out and stomped

her foot. "I am not cute. Cute is for babies! And don't call me 'sweetie'! You're a dum-dum!"

The class erupted in laughter. "You tell her, kid!" Gabriel said, applauding.

"You're a dum-dum too!" the tot fired back.

"I'd like you all to meet your client," Mr. Kaye said, trying to calm everyone down. "This is Miss Cordelia Vanderweil. If we could keep the name-calling to a minimum, Cordy, dear?"

"As in Victoria Vanderweil? The famous fashion designer who practically launched the designer-jean craze in the seventies?" South asked.

"The one and only," Mr. Kaye replied. "This precious young lady is her granddaughter."

Cordelia looked over the crowd of faces staring at her. "My grandma isn't gonna like any of you," she said. "You're all mean and icky!"

South flinched. "I've been called a lot of things before, but never 'icky'!"

"You don't mean that," Mr. Kaye insisted, taking the child's hand. "These lovely students are going to design you a pretty dress for your fifth birthday party." He then turned to face the class. "And your granny is going to be the judge of who wins this challenge, after Cordy has selected her top two."

"No way!" Mars exclaimed. "Victoria Vanderweil is going to grade our designs? That is amazing!"

"Well, that depends," Mr. Kaye pointed out, "on how amazing your designs are."

"My birthday is Valentine's Day," Cordy revealed proudly. "My granny says it's because I'm so lovable."

Mickey raised her hand. "What are the guidelines for the dress?"

"You will have to ask Miss Cordelia that," Mr. Kaye replied. "Cordy, they're all yours."

"I want a fancy dress," the child rattled off. "With bows and pearl buttons! Oh, and balloons!"

Gabriel raised an eyebrow. "You want balloons on the dress—or attached to it?"

Cordelia waved her hand dismissively. "I like

pink and purple and red and yellow and orange and blue. I like twirly ballerinas. Oh! And the Easter Bunny!"

Mickey scratched her head. This was a tall order to fill! "You mean these are your favorite things you want at your party? Or things you want us to think about when designing your dress?"

"Rainbows! I love rainbows and spaghetti!"

"Do you all think you have enough information?" Mr. Kaye asked the class. "I do believe Cordelia has lunch at the Plaza Hotel with her granny shortly."

"You better do a good job!" she said, leaving them with a stern warning. "Or else!"

"I second that," Mr. Kaye said. "You have one week to complete your challenge. Good luck— you'll need it."

When Mickey got home from school, she pulled out her sketchbook and began drawing. But instead of a party dress, she found herself doodling a hot air balloon with Cordy and the Easter Bunny sitting in it. They were eating a bowl of spaghetti and meatballs as the balloon wafted in the clouds.

There was no way she was going to mess up an assignment again—scoring a two was not an option. So she decided to call JC. If he could whip up clothes for his Chihuahua Madonna, maybe he'd have some ideas of how to design for a temperamental tot.

"Wow, that's quite a wish list to fill," he said, listening intently as Mickey rattled off all of Cordy's requirements. "Where does the spaghetti come in?"

"I don't have any idea," Mickey said. "I was thinking petals of different-colored fabric for the ball-gown skirt, tulle underneath, and short puffed sleeves that are balloon-like. Then a faux-fur stole that looks like a bunny rabbit?"

"Like I said, where does the spaghetti come in?"

Mickey flopped back on her pillow and closed her eyes. "I just don't see how I can work it into the design. It doesn't go. Everything is light and fluffy; spaghetti is long and slippery."

"What about the accessories? Maybe you can put a plate of spaghetti on Cordy's darling little head?" JC suggested.

"You're not helping," Mickey moaned. "This is a huge challenge. Victoria Vanderweil is going to see my design."

"I say ditch the pasta and make her a purse instead."

Suddenly, a lightbulb went off over Mickey's head.

"Say that again!"

"Ditch the pasta?"

"No!" Mickey exclaimed. "The part about making her a purse. JC, you're a genius!"

"That I am," her friend replied. "That I am."

Cordy the Critic

A week later, it was time for the big reveal: Cordy's fifth birthday outfit as designed by FAB's students. Mars was eager to present hers, and her hand shot up as soon as Mr. Kaye asked for volunteers.

"Ooh! Ooh! Me! Me!" she said, wheeling her dress form right in front of Cordy. The little girl was licking a blue raspberry lollipop and seemed bored.

"So I call this 'High Five,'" Mars explained to Cordy. "See? The print is made out of the number five in all sizes and colors. I used it for the mini-skirt and the matching hoodie. How cool is that?"

Cordy yawned. "I hate it," she said, taking her lolly and tossing it at the mannequin. It stuck to the hem of the skirt, and Mars gasped in horror.

"I know my ABCs and my numbers," Cordy continued. "I don't watch *Sesame Street* anymore!"

Mr. Kaye nodded. "She does have a point, Mars. Perhaps the dress is too juvenile?"

"She's five," Mars groaned. "Not twenty-five."

"It's icky," Cordy insisted. "Blech! Take it away."

Mars wheeled her design back to her desk and sunk down in her seat.

"That kid is a nightmare," she said to Mickey. "Thanks to her, I'm probably going to fail this assignment."

"Gabriel," Mr. Kaye summoned. "You're next."

"Hey, Cordelia," Gabriel said, uncovering his design with a flourish. "I think you're really going to like what I made for you."

"Doubt it," Cordy replied. "I hate boys."

"But you love balloons, right?" he said.

Cordy's ears perked up. "Yeah."

He spun the form around to reveal a volumi-nous party dress trimmed in white lace. It had a huge cream-colored balloon-like skirt made from layers of chiffon. "Ta-da!"

Cordy wrinkled her nose. "Where's the balloon?"

Gabriel fluffed the skirt out even more. "Right here! See, it's big and billowy like a balloon."

"I don't like it." Cordy sniffed. "It looks like a marshmallow. And marshmallows make me pukey."

"Oh, dear," Mr. Kaye said. "We don't want our client nauseated. I'm afraid it's not good news for you, Gabriel."

South's design was next. "I think of it as 'Street Ballerina,'" she said, explaining the tutu she'd made, trimmed with silver grommets. "And since you said you love rainbows, I did the ballerina tank top in a silver hologram fabric that reflects the light." She tilted the mannequin so it cast shimmering rainbow prisms on the wall.

Cordy stood up and surveyed the dress. "It's kinda nice," she said. "But what if it's raining? Or it's my bedtime? Where do the rainbows go?"

"I guess you have to carry a flashlight with you," South replied, annoyed. "Give me a break. This outfit is awesome. I'd wear it."

"Well, you are not the client," Mr. Kaye reminded her. "Cordy, thumbs up or thumbs down?"

Instead, Cordy curled up in a ball in Mr. Kaye's desk chair and stuck her thumb in her mouth.

"Moving on then," their teacher said. "Mickey, let's see what you've come up with."

Mickey took a deep breath and rolled her dress form toward the front of the room. She smiled at Cordy, who looked like she needed a nap.

"So I had a long talk with the Easter Bunny," Mickey began.

Cordy's eyes flew open. "You did?"

"I did. Peter Cottontail and I go way back. He even helped me make this white rabbit fur wrap for you—faux bunny fur, of course." She removed the cropped jacket from the mannequin and draped it around Cordy's shoulders.

"Ooh," Cordy cooed. "Soft."

"You'll notice that the dress that goes with it is very *fancy*," Mickey said, choosing her words carefully. She had to convince Cordy that she had given her exactly what she asked for. "The little puff sleeves are inspired by party balloons, and there are pearl buttons down the back and a big pink bow at the waist. The handkerchief skirt is made out of rainbow-colored silk dupioni, and you'll notice that if you twirl in it…" She spun the dress form around in a circle. "It's very ballerina."

Cordy was taking it all in, admiring all the details that Mickey had designed just for her. "You forgot the spaghetti," she said suddenly. "I said I wanted spaghetti."

From her backpack, Mickey pulled out a gold-fringed cross-body bag. The fringe looked like long strands of spaghetti. "You'll see that I even gave you a meatball," she said, pointing to the large red wooden bead she'd fastened onto the clasp. "I didn't forget your spaghetti."

"Gimme!" Cordy said, snatching the purse out of Mickey's hands.

"Well, that's a positive review," Mr. Kaye said. "Good job, Mickey. Your client is pleased. South, you were Cordy's other top choice, so you both will be presenting your designs to Victoria Vanderweil."

"Yes!" South fist-pumped the air. "She shoots… She scores!"

Mickey tried to contain her excitement—at least until she could find JC at lunch in the cafeteria and share the news with him.

"Thank you, Mr. Kaye," she said modestly. "And thank you too, Cordy."

Cordy was too busy stuffing her new purse with pens, pencils, and erasers from inside Mr. Kaye's desk drawer.

"Do you think I could put real spaghetti in here?" she asked him.

"Why don't you go to the cafeteria and find out?" he suggested, giving the youngster a gentle push toward Mickey. "I don't have any more pencils left—or patience for that matter. Besides, I'm

sure your two favorite designers won't mind taking you to lunch."

South's draw dropped. "Me? I don't babysit."

"*I'm not a baby!*" Cordy exploded. "And
nobody sits on me."

"Well, could we just be lunch buddies then?"
Mickey asked her. She tried to take Cordy's hand,
but the child was slippery.

"I want mac and cheese!" Cordy yelled as she
bolted out of the classroom. "And chocolate milk!
And chicken dinos!"

Before Mickey could say another word, Cordy
took off in a sprint down the hallway.

"Good heavens!" Mr. Kaye shouted. "Stop her!

Victoria Vanderweil's grandchild is on the loose
and I'm responsible for her. Go find her...*now*!"

Cafeteria Chaos

Mickey raced after Cordy, but it was too late. The fourth-period bell had rung, and the hallway was now flooded with students. Finding a little girl in this crowd was like searching for a needle in a haystack.

"Have you seen a kid?" she asked as she collided with Jade and her brother, Jake, at their lockers.

"A kid? As opposed to what—an alien life-form?" Jake replied, snickering. "There are kids everywhere."

"No, I mean a little kid. Five years old, curly blond hair, bad attitude."

"Maybe you should file a missing person's report," Jade suggested, smiling sweetly. "Need a hand?"

Mickey had learned by now that anytime Jade was nice, she was either faking it—or had an ulterior motive.

"No, thanks. I'll find her myself!"

"What's that all about?" Jade asked her brother as Mickey dashed down the three flights of stairs to the cafeteria, hoping that Cordy had followed her nose.

"Gabriel texted me that Mr. Kaye is freaking out.

He put Mickey in charge of Victoria Vanderweil's grandkid," Jake replied.

"Then she must be in *big* trouble," Jade said, checking her lipstick in her locker mirror before shutting the door. "That's the best news I've heard all day."

JC spotted Mickey running in circles in the cafeteria and waved from their regular table.

"Hey, can't have lunch. Gotta find a missing kid," she said breathlessly.

JC pointed under the table. "You mean

this missing kid?" There was Cordy, sitting cross-legged on the floor and feeding JC's dog, Madonna, scraps of her grilled cheese sandwich. The tiny dog was dressed in a purple cashmere sweater with a monogram *M* on it. JC made sure she was always dressed to puppy perfection.

"How did you know?" Mickey gasped.

"The spaghetti-and-meatball purse kind of gave her away," JC said, winking. "I thought maybe someone might be missing her. I didn't think it would be you."

"I know." Mickey sat down at the table and wiped her brow with a paper napkin. "Mr. Kaye kind of put me on babysitting duty."

"I'm not a baby!" shouted a voice under the table.

"Right! Not a baby!" Mickey quickly retracted her statement for fear that Cordy would bolt again. "I'm on *lunch buddy* duty."

"That's better," Cordy said, giving Madonna a belly rub on the cafeteria floor.

JC peered under the table. "Remember what I told you. Doggie is a secret. She's not allowed to come to school."

"I love Doggie!" Cordy said, scooping the tiny dog into her arms. "Shhh!"

JC offered Mickey half of his sandwich. "Did Mr. Kaye like your design?"

"More importantly, the little princess did." She

motioned under the table. "I get to present my look to Victoria Vanderweil at her design studio."

"Awesomeness!" JC cheered, dipping a fry in a puddle of ketchup. "You're the best designer at FAB, in my humble opinion. I told you the last assignment was just a temporary setback."

"Aww, thanks." Mickey blushed. "But if I don't get Cordy back to Mr. Kaye's studio, it will be a permanent setback. You should have seen Mr. Kaye. He was red in the face, and I think steam was coming out of his ears."

"Not to worry," JC assured her. "Everyone is safe and sound. You're welcome."

But before she could thank him, Mickey caught

a glimpse of something out of the corner of her eye. It was Cordy. She had taken Madonna in JC's purple quilted tote bag and was making a run for it.

"JC! Look!" Mickey cried. "She's getting away!"

JC stared in horror. "And she dognapped my Madonna!"

He leaped to his feet and stood on top of the table to get a bird's-eye view of Cordy's escape route. There were students everywhere in line with their lunch trays, and it was almost impossible to follow the blond curls fleeing for the exit.

"Stop, thief! Come back!" JC yelled.

Mickey was already on Cordy's heels. "Wait, Cordy! You didn't have your ice-cream sundae for dessert," she said, trying to reason with the little girl. "Lots of whipped cream and sprinkles!"

"I hate whipped cream!" Cordy fired back, and she pushed a garbage can in Mickey's way. "More than I hate marshmallows!"

Mickey ran straight into it, and the can spilled over, showering her in discarded meat loaf and mashed potatoes.

"Hah, hah! You made a messy!" Cordy chuckled, making a beeline for the cafeteria exit.

"Wait! Stop her!" JC yelled, pushing his way

through the cafeteria lines and knocking over trays of food in his wake. "I got her! I got her!"

He dove for her, but Cordy was too fast. She sidestepped him just in the nick of time, and JC landed with a hard *splat* on the tile floor. Cordy disappeared—with Madonna—out of the cafeteria.

Mickey helped him to his feet. "I told you she was slippery."

"Slippery? She's worse than a snake wearing sunscreen! Where do you think she would go?"

Mickey tried to put herself in a five-year-old's shoes. But then again, Cordy was no average five-year-old. "Somewhere where she could play with Madonna…or dress her up."

"You thinking what I'm thinking?" JC suddenly caught on.

"The runway!" they both shouted in unison.

Seeing Spots

Mickey and JC raced to the bottom floor of FAB where the auditorium housed a gigantic runway stage used for the Runway Showdown. The doors were locked.

"That's strange," JC reflected. "The auditorium is always open."

"Unless someone locked it from the inside," Mickey said. "Cordy is so smart. She knew we'd figure out where she was going and was trying to slow us down."

"We'll have to pick the lock," JC said, rummaging in his pockets. "I don't suppose you have a pick on you?"

Mickey dug in her bag and pulled out one of the safety pins that had fallen off her No Sew assignment fiasco. "Will this do?"

"Perfect!" JC said, squatting down on his knees and jabbing the lock with the sharp end of the pin. "When I was six, I got locked in the bathroom of my day camp and had to use a paper clip to get out."

Mickey nodded. "So you're a pro at breaking and entering?"

With a few clicks, the lock sprung open. JC smiled. "You could say that."

They pushed open the door. The lights were off, but they could hear noises coming from backstage.

"Tiptoe," Mickey warned him. "We don't want to scare her."

"Scare her? You think anything scares that tiny terror? She scares me!"

"You look so pretty in pink, don't you think?" They heard a little voice behind the curtains.

Madonna responded with a few yelps.

"If she hurts my dog…" JC said through gritted teeth.

"What's wrong, Doggie? You don't like my dress?"

Mickey gently pulled back the curtain. There, wrapped in a long piece of pink chiffon, was Madonna. Cordy was doing her best to coax her down the runway, but the dog's legs were tangled in the fabric.

"She doesn't wanna model," the little girl said with a huff. "Bad doggie."

"No, she's not a bad doggie. She just has a strong sense of personal style—like someone else I know," Mickey said. She gently picked Madonna up and unraveled her from the outfit Cordy had "designed." She handed the dog back to JC, who heaved a huge sigh of relief.

"What's wrong with my dress?" Cordy asked,

tears welling in her eyes. "I found it there." She pointed to a huge bin of discarded scrap material. "Why does Doggie hate it?"

JC saw how upset she was and forgot to be angry. "You did a beautiful gown for Madonna," he said, sitting down next to her. "But she prefers minidresses over maxis. More room for her to move around." He took the pink fabric and folded it in half, draping it over Madonna's back and ears. "See?"

Madonna scampered around in her new look approvingly.

"Oh, she's so pretty!" Cordy clapped her hands together.

"Maybe you could come over to JC's house for a playdate and design more clothes for her," Mickey suggested.

JC shot her a look. The last thing he wanted was Cordy invading his home design studio. "Yeah, or maybe not…"

"Tomorrow?" Cordy begged. "Can I come over tomorrow?"

JC shook his head. "Ya know, I have a lot of homework and a really hard science test to study for…"

"Tomorrow would be perfect," Mickey said, giving him a little kick.

"Ouch! Says who?"

"Cordy, do you think you could introduce JC to your grandma? Show him what you *both* are making for Madonna?"

"Oh yes," Cordy replied. "Granny Vicky has a doggie too. Her name is Princess Puffynose."

JC rolled his eyes. "Granny Vicky?" he whispered to Mickey. "Princess Puffynose? Seriously?"

"I think you should design some new dog clothes that would wow Victoria Vanderweil," Mickey insisted. "How cool would it be to have your canine couture on her personal pup?"

JC thought for a moment. "Mickey, did I ever tell you you're a genius?"

Mickey smiled. "So it's a date, Cordy. You, me,

JC, and Madonna—and Granny Vicky. I'm sure Mr. Kaye would be happy to set it up."

JC watched as Cordy, now on all fours, chased Madonna down the runway. "I can hardly wait," he said.

When a black stretch limo pulled up in front of JC's apartment building after school the next day, he and Mickey had no doubt who was inside.

"Your playdate has arrived," Mickey teased him, peering out the window. A chauffeur escorted Cordy out of the car, into the elevator, and to the front door—which Cordy pounded on. "I'm here! I'm here! Open up!"

As JC unlocked the front door, she pushed past him and headed straight into his bedroom and design space. "Where's my puppy?"

"*Your* puppy?" JC exclaimed. "Do you want to rephrase that?"

"She's a five-year-old." Mickey tried to calm him.

"With a talent for dognapping," JC reminded her. "I'm not taking my eyes off her for a second." He locked the front door to the apartment and bolted it.

"So," Mickey said, joining Cordy, "what

kind of outfit should you and JC make for Princess Puffynose?"

"She likes polka dots," Cordy replied. "Blue and yellow polka dots."

"Uh-huh," JC said, taking notes in his sketch-book. "What else?"

"Ruffles. Oh, and shiny shoes."

"We are talking about a dog, right?" JC asked her. "Not a circus clown?"

Cordy stamped her foot. "Polka dots."

"KK, not a problem," JC said. "Polka dots it is."

After carefully selecting a cream-colored cashmere fabric from his box of scraps, JC cut out a pattern, stitched it together, and held it up for Cordy to see.

"Where are the polka dots?" she asked stubbornly.

"Relax, I haven't gotten to that part yet."

He handed the little girl a box of sequins. "Pick out the dots you like, and I'll sew them on."

"Ooh, this one!" Cordy said, digging in and selecting a large sapphire-blue one. "And this one." She picked out a sparkling canary yellow.

"Nice," JC said, attaching them to the dog sweater. "This kid's got an eye for color."

Cordy handed JC sequin after sequin until the sweater was covered in shimmering "dots."

"It's beautiful," Mickey said, admiring JC's handiwork. "Never mind Princess Puffynose. *I'd* wear that sweater."

JC slipped it over Madonna's tiny head. "Madonna, model please," he said. Madonna obeyed, prancing around the room.

Cordy giggled with delight. "Let's go show Granny Vicky!" she said, tugging on Mickey's arm.

"Now? You want to go show her now?" Mickey gasped. "But we're not ready."

"Now!" Cordy commanded and marched out of the room with Madonna scampering after her. She stood at the front door. "Open up," she said, pointing to the lock.

"Let me get my coat and Madonna's leash," JC said, excited. "Granny Vicky, here we come."

8

★ An Audience with the Queen ★

The chauffeur drove them straight to Victoria Vanderweil's design studio in the heart of the Fashion District.

"Do you think she'll be okay with us arriving unannounced?" Mickey whispered to JC.

"Do we have a choice?" He pointed to Cordy, who was anxiously hanging out the window of the limo with Madonna.

"We're here!" she said, as the car pulled up in front of a large building.

"Follow me," Cordy said, taking Mickey by the hand. "I know where it is."

Inside the building, Cordy cheerfully waved to the security guard and walked them straight to the elevator bank.

"Press the eight button," she instructed JC.

"Yes, ma'am," JC replied.

When the elevator opened, Cordy led them down a long hallway to a door with gold letters on it. It read "House of V."

Mickey took a deep breath. "My palms are sweating," she whispered to JC.

Before he could respond, Cordy opened the door and bounded inside, marching past the receptionist at the front desk and straight into the studio. "Granny Vicky!" she called. "Come see, come see!"

"Sorry!" Mickey apologized, running after Cordy.

Inside the studio, a petite woman with silvery gray hair pinned in a bun emerged from behind a rack of clothing. She was dressed in a dark pair of jeans, a white sweater, and a chic black blazer.

Mickey elbowed JC in the ribs. "It's her!" she whispered. "I think I'm gonna faint!"

JC nodded. "Oh good. You can break my fall when I pass out after you."

"Cordelia! What are you doing here?" Victoria asked, surprised.

Mickey cleared her throat. "Ahem, we brought her," she said. "Me…him…her…" She realized she wasn't making any sense.

"Who are you?" the designer asked.

"Oh! I'm Mickey Williams, and this is my friend Javen Cumberland."

"She means Kenzie Wills and JC Canine Couture designs," JC jumped in. "We're designers—from the Fashion Academy of Brooklyn."

"Ah, yes," the woman said. "Chester Kaye's students."

"Yes! Yes! Chester's students," Mickey tried her

94

hardest not to giggle at her teacher's funny first name. "I won the challenge for designing a party dress for Cordy, and JC—"

"Made a sweater with your darling granddaughter for your dog, Princess Puffynose!" JC jumped in. He scooped up Madonna and held her in front of Victoria's face so she could get a good look.

"Lovely workmanship," she said, fingering the sweater and scratching Madonna between the ears. "There's just one small problem."

"What? I can fix it!" JC replied.

"Can you make it about eight sizes larger?"

JC looked confused. "Is Princess Puffynose a dog or a grizzly bear?"

"A Dalmatian," Victoria said, finding a silver framed photo on her desk and showing it to him. "A fifty-two-pound one, to be exact."

"Oh." JC's heart sunk. "I see where the polka dot part came from. Cordy, did you forget to tell us that Puffynose is a *big* doggie?"

"And her name is Prudence. Cordelia had trouble saying that when she was a baby, so she called her Puffynose."

Mickey nodded. "Gotcha. I couldn't say my grandma Barbara's name when I was little so I called her Boo-Boo."

"Boo-Boo! That's funny!" Cordy cracked up.

JC was mortified. "This sweater will never fit Prudence. I'm so sorry."

Victoria brushed it off with a wave of her hand. "Not to worry. Prudy isn't much of a fashionista anyway. My granddaughter, however, is." She playfully ruffled Cordy's curls. "And she told me all about your design for her party dress. I can't wait to see it."

Mickey's heart jumped in her chest. "Really? I can't wait to show it to you! Cordy is going to look so pretty for her birthday party."

Victoria smiled. "Did you have fun with these two lovely young students, Cordelia, dear?"

"Yes!" Cordy replied enthusiastically. "Can they buddy sit me again?"

"I think she means B-A-B-Y sit her," Mickey spelled.

"I don't see why not," Victoria said, taking an invitation off her desk and handing it to Mickey. "Why don't you meet me here Saturday at noon? I was planning on bringing Cordy since she loves fancy parties so much. It would be very helpful to have an extra pair of eyes or two watching her."

"You're not kidding," JC muttered under his breath.

Mickey looked at the invite. "OMG! Really? We can come?" It was an invitation to a luncheon given by the Women Designers of America Association.

"Why yes," Victoria replied. "A good friend of mine is receiving the WDAA Achievement Award, and I'm introducing her."

"We are so there," JC said, snatching the invitation out of Mickey's hands.

"Excellent!" Victoria said. "Cordy and I will expect you."

9

Surprise Guests

Mickey tried on a third outfit and looked in the full-length mirror in Aunt Olive's room. "I don't know," she said, studying the navy-blue sheath from every angle. She'd paired the simple knee-length dress with a gold chain-link belt and black platform loafers. "It just doesn't feel right. It's too stuffy." Frustrated, she flopped down on Olive's bed.

"What is it you always tell me? Fashion speaks

volumes?" Olive asked. "What do you want your look to say?"

"That I belong at a WDAA luncheon. That I'm destined to be a member of their club one day because I have my own strong sense of style."

"Then say that," Olive said, poking her. "I know you can."

Once again, Mickey disappeared into her closet and rummaged through the racks. This time, she chose a purple silk blouse and a black suede mini-skirt with a fringed hem. When she pulled on a pair of tall leather boots and gold hoop earrings, the entire outfit came together.

"By George, I think she's got it!" Olive teased

when Mickey came into her room to model. "Just one more thing…"

She pulled out her purple cashmere trapeze jacket and handed it to her niece.

"Oh, Aunt Olive. This is perfect! Are you sure? It's so expensive."

"I'm sure." Olive beamed. "Go get 'em!"

When Mickey arrived at the hotel where the luncheon was being held, JC was already out front waiting for her. He was wearing a chocolate-brown velvet suit and a pink tie.

"Don't we look stylish?" he asked, offering his arm like a gentleman. "Shall we?"

Mickey giggled. "Do you really think we can

pull this off?" she asked. "I mean, we're just fashion students—not world-famous designers."

"Speak for yourself," JC teased. He pulled a Sharpie marker out of his pocket. "I'm ready to sign autographs."

They walked in and gave their names at the check-in table. "Yes, you're guests of Ms. Vanderweil," the woman replied. "Go right in."

The private banquet room was decked out with red-and-gold table linens, sparkling crystal, and enormous floral centerpieces. All the guests were dressed to the nines in the most fabulously fashionable attire, and the room was filled with famous designers, supermodels, and celebrities.

"OMG!" JC said, grabbing her arm. "Is that Isaac Mizrahi? I'm gonna faint!"

Mickey steadied him. "I'm sure anyone who's anyone in fashion will be here," she whispered. "We have to stay cool and calm." Just then, Heidi Klum strolled by and Mickey practically fell over. "Heidi. It's Heidi!"

"So much for calm and cool," JC said.

But before they could mingle with the *Project Runway* host and judge, Cordy found them. "You're here! Come color with me!" she said, dragging Mickey by the hand to her table.

A frazzled-looking banquet manager had given her a stack of paper and some crayons and was delighted that reinforcements had arrived. "Yes!" the woman practically cheered. "Please go color with her."

"Um, sure," Mickey said as Heidi disappeared into the crowd. "What are we drawing, Cordy?"

Cordy handed her a red crayon. "A princess in a castle roller-skating with a penguin," she replied. "And they're eating pepperoni pizza at midnight."

JC raised an eyebrow. "This kid's got some imagination."

"She kinda reminds me of me when I was her age," Mickey told him. "I used to give my Barbie dolls extreme makeovers."

She sat down and began to sketch. "No, make her dress longer," Cordy instructed. "And she needs a crown—and pearls."

Mickey obeyed. "Pearls, of course. Every princess needs pearls." She noticed that Cordy had a strand of delicate pink ones around her neck.

"Do you see Ms. Vanderweil anywhere?" Mickey asked JC.

"Negative. But I'm pretty sure that's Betsey Johnson over there chatting up Isaac."

"Great," Mickey groaned. She desperately wanted to go meet all the famous designers in the room, but Cordy insisted they stay by her side and color.

"I have an idea," JC whispered to Mickey. He turned to Cordy. "So, who wants to go and get some cookies?"

The little girl's eyes lit up. "Cookies? Where?"

"Over there." JC motioned to the far corner of the room. "I know I saw a waiter with a big, silver tray of pink-sprinkled cookies shaped like shoes."

"Where?" Cordy stood on her chair. "I don't see him."

"Well, let's go find him then," Mickey said, following JC's lead. "Let's go get the cookie guy."

Cordy was already several steps in front of them yelling, "Cookie guy! Cookie guy!"

"Brilliant," she said to JC. "The pink-sprinkle part was the best."

Cordy was already cutting through the crowd, and they did their best to follow her.

"Excuse me. Pardon me," JC said, elbowing his way through. He accidentally bumped a man's arm and spilled his drink. "Oops! My bad!" JC exclaimed as the guest turned around and glared.

It was Isaac!

"Mr. Mizrahi." JC practically bowed in his presence. "You are my fashion idol. I wanna be you!"

Isaac helped him stand up. "Darling, be yourself! There's already plenty of me out there."

JC found Mickey peeking under tablecloths in search of Cordy. "Pinch me!" he pleaded with her. "I just talked to Isaac."

Mickey sighed. "Great. You're meeting fashion royalty, and I'm on my knees crawling around looking for Cordy."

"There you two are," said a voice behind them. It was Victoria. "What are you doing on the floor?" she asked, confused.

"Shoes! I love shoes!" Mickey quickly covered. "I was just admiring everyone's under the table. Ooh, look! Jimmy Choo!"

"I'd prefer you to keep your eyes on my grand-daughter and make sure she behaves."

"Not to worry," Mickey reassured her. "We're on Cordy patrol."

Victoria looked around. "Where is she?"

Mickey swallowed hard. "Where is she? She's…she's…"

"She's coloring at your table," JC fibbed. "We just went to get her some prettier colors—cornflower blue and cotton candy." There was no way they could tell Victoria that her granddaughter was up to her disappearing tricks again.

"Fine, but don't leave her alone for too long," Victoria warned them.

"We know," Mickey said. "Believe me, we know."

A voice over the loudspeaker announced the start

of the luncheon program. "Ladies and gentlemen, if you would kindly take your seats. We'll begin."

"That's my cue," Victoria said. "I'm introducing the honoree."

"Have fun," JC said, waving. He pulled Mickey aside. "We have to find Little Miss Tiny Terror before Granny gets back to her seat."

"Look!" Mickey said. She spotted a pink ruffled dress darting between guests a few feet away by the stage. "I think I see her."

A security guard jumped in front of them. "Seats, please."

"But, we can't—not just yet," Mickey tried to explain.

"Seats," the guard repeated. There was no way he was letting them through.

"Fine," Mickey told him. "But you'll be sorry."

They returned to their table, hoping Cordy would be escorted back as well.

"Might as well enjoy ourselves," JC said, helping himself to a basket of rolls and butter. He glanced down at the program on his plate and skimmed it. "Oh no." He gasped. "Do you know who the honoree is? The person Victoria is introducing?"

"Shh!" Mickey hushed him. Victoria was onstage, clearing her throat.

"There is not a single person in this room—I

daresay in the world—who does not know the name Bridget Lee…"

Mickey's mouth dropped. "Bridget Lee? As in Jade and Jake Lee's mother?"

JC shoved the program under her nose. "That's what I was trying to tell you."

Victoria continued. "Her designs are exquisite, as is the woman herself. Without further ado, I give you this year's WDAA honoree, my dear friend, Bridget Lee."

There was thunderous applause, then Bridget took the stage with Jade and Jake by her side. "I am so honored," she said, kissing Victoria on both cheeks. "Next to being a mother, I consider my fashion label my proudest achievement."

Suddenly, the lights went out and the entire ballroom was pitch-black.

JC and Mickey had the same thought at the same time: *Cordy!*

There were gasps and cries from the audience. "Don't panic, everyone," Victoria called from the stage. "I'm sure it's just a fuse and the lights will come on shortly."

Mickey knew better. "I'm going to find her," she whispered to JC. She headed toward Victoria's voice, feeling her way through the tables. "Cordy?" she whispered. "Cordy, what did you do?"

She thought she heard giggling coming from the right side of the room and made her way in that direction. She got down on all fours and called the little troublemaker again. "Cordy? Come out, come out wherever you are!"

When a few lights flickered back on, Mickey realized she was on the floor, staring at someone's stunning pink stilettos.

"May I help you?" Heidi Klum bent down and asked her.

"Me? No, I'm good. Nice shoes!" She was mortified but managed to stand up, dust herself off, and continue toward the electrical closet down the hall. Inside, she found Cordy standing on a stool, flipping switches on the lighting panel for the ballroom.

"Cordy! What are you doing?" she asked, pulling the little girl down. "You could fall and hurt yourself."

"I'm playing hide-and-seek," she replied. "I win."

Mickey turned the lights back on, then took Cordy firmly by the hand. "Yes, you win! Let's go back to the table and get your prize."

"What is it?" Cordy asked excitedly. "Is it a dolly? Or a puppy?"

"You'll have to come with me and find out," Mickey said, trying her best not to disrupt the presentation any further. Jade and Jake were standing onstage beaming as Bridget went on and on about her long career as a designer for Hollywood's elite.

"What did I miss?" she asked JC. She pulled Cordy on her lap and locked her arms around the child's waist.

"Oh, praise be to Lady Gaga." JC heaved a sigh of relief. "You got her back."

"Where's my prize?" Cordy demanded. "I want my prize."

JC looked confused. "What did *I* miss?"

"Cordy won our hide-and-seek game, so I promised her a prize," Mickey explained. "Any ideas?"

JC pulled a Chihuahua-sized shiny rhinestone

dog collar out of his pocket. "How about a diamond bracelet?" he asked Cordy.

"Oooh! Yes!" Cordy said, grabbing it out of his fingertips. She put it on her wrist and waved it in the air.

"Look, Granny Vicky!" she shouted at the stage. "I got a diamond bracelet! Look, everybody! Look what I got!"

Mickey's cheeks flushed bright red. The entire audience was now staring in her direction, and Bridget Lee was speechless. Jade was the only one smiling—she looked like a cat that had swallowed a canary.

Mickey hoped Victoria had a good sense

of humor and would wave back at her granddaughter. Instead, she stood by Bridget, furrowing her brow and pursing her lips tightly. Then she motioned for Cordy to zip hers as well.

"Granny's not happy," JC whispered to Mickey.

"Just my luck," Mickey said, sighing. "Tomorrow is the day South and I present our designs."

Cordy went back to coloring and the program continued, but Mickey had a sinking feeling this WDAA luncheon would be her last.

Not O-Kaye

"Explain it to me again," Mr. Kaye said, rubbing his temples. "You lost Victoria Vanderweil's granddaughter, who then shut off the lights on the most important fashion-industry luncheon of the season?"

"You forgot the part where Cordy stopped the show by yelling at her granny onstage," Mickey said. "It was an epic disaster."

"So I heard," Mr. Kaye replied. He had

summoned Mickey and JC to his office early Monday morning to get their side of their story. He'd received a furious email from Bridget Lee.

"Such a disgraceful show of ill manners should be severely reprimanded," he read. "I demand that your two FAB students be suspended for their actions."

"Suspended?" Mickey shouted. "That's so unfair!"

"That's so Jade," JC piped up. "You know she put her mother up to this."

"I'm sure that's true," Mr. Kaye said, "and I think suspension is a bit extreme. But I'm very disappointed in both of you. You should have been watching Cordelia like a hawk."

"But Isaac Mizrahi was there," JC tried to explain. "And Heidi Klum. It was like I died and went to fashion heaven."

"Which is why you failed to do your assigned task," Mr. Kaye said sternly. "It's not an excuse."

"It won't happen again," Mickey said, pleading with him. "We promise. We'll do better next time."

"What makes you so sure there will be a next time?" Mr. Kaye replied. "I was planning on having you and South report to Ms. Vanderweil this week with your designs for Cordy's dress. But from the sound of things, that's off the table."

"What do you mean?" Mickey asked.

Mr. Kaye adjusted his reading glasses. "My

dear friend Vicky Vanderweil was so mortified that she has decided the only two students she can trust from FAB are my own twins, Jade and Jake. They will be presenting *their* designs to her this week, and she will choose one of them for Cordy to wear."

Mickey didn't know what to say. So JC spoke for her. "That's the biggest pile of puppy poop I've ever heard!" he exclaimed.

Mr. Kaye frowned. "Mr. Cumberland, do remember whom you are speaking to."

"JC's right," Mickey added. "It's just not fair—not to me, not to South. We worked hard on those dresses for Cordy."

"I understand your feelings," Mr. Kaye said. "But I also understand how embarrassed Ms. Lee and Ms. Vanderweil were at this VIP event. There may be nothing more I can do about it. As for the two of you…"

Mickey and JC gulped. "You are representing FAB, and this is your first and last warning: do not embarrass me again."

South was equally angry when Mickey broke the news to her before class.

"So you blew *both* our chances? Thanks a lot!"

she said, storming off. Mickey felt awful, and there didn't seem to be any way she could fix the situation. She found a quiet corner on the front steps of the school and called her mom.

"Aww, honey, that stinks." Her mother was trying to make her feel better. "That Jade girl sounds like a real backstabber."

"She is. And I really didn't do anything wrong. Cordy is just such a handful!"

"Sounds like someone I know." Her mom chuckled.

"What do you mean?"

"When you were three years old, I took you to Wanamaker's with me. It was Bring Your

Daughter to Work Day," her mom explained. "While I was helping a client pick a mascara at my cosmetics counter, you got loose in my makeup kit and colored the entire wall at Wanamaker's with eyeshadow and lipstick. You drew a huge rainbow and a field of flowers."

"OMG, did you get in big trouble?"

"I did. My boss was furious, but then a bunch of shoppers liked your mural and the store decided to keep it up for six months. You inspired a whole new look for the cosmetics section."

Mickey thought for a moment. "So I was as crazy as Cordy?"

"I wouldn't call it crazy. I would call it *colorful*.

It sounds like you two really get each other. You're a great role model for her, Mickey Mouse. So don't let Jade or anyone else get in the way, KK?"

Mickey smiled. "KK."

She found JC at his locker, looking sad and discouraged. "I know what might cheer you up," she said.

"Front row tix to a Madonna concert?" JC asked hopefully.

"Not quite. But how do you feel about crashing a five-year-old's birthday party?"

11

Party Girl

Mickey was sure it wouldn't be hard to figure out where Victoria was throwing her granddaughter's birthday bash. All she had to do was think like Cordy. She and JC met up after school to do some Web research.

"I'm googling and getting nothing," JC said, scanning the Web on his laptop for any hint of where and when the party was taking place.

"We know it's next weekend because Cordy

said her b-day was Valentine's Day," Mickey said, thinking out loud. "And we know how much Cordy likes sweets."

"Bingo!" JC said, showing her his computer screen. "The Annual Vanderweil Valentine's Day Fete at Dolly's Candy Bar. Saturday at eleven a.m."

"That has to be it," Mickey agreed. "How do we get in?"

JC scanned the article. "It says 'By Invitation Only.'"

"Then we need to borrow someone's invitation."

"Who?" JC scratched his head. "I don't know any fashionable five-year-olds."

"Who else would be coming?" Mickey asked. "What about the press?"

JC suddenly grinned from ear to ear. "How do you feel about being a fashion blogger?" he asked. With a few strokes of his computer keyboard and mouse, he whipped up an authentic-looking press badge and printed it out for Mickey.

"Kenzie Wills, Fashion Blogger?" she read. "Do you really think I can get away with this?"

"Just flash your badge. No one will know," JC said. "At least it will get you close to the front door. Then you just have to find Cordy and have her help you get back into Granny's good graces."

Mickey had counted on the party being crowded, but she never expected one hundred–plus kids and their fashionable moms to be storming the doors of Dolly's Candy Bar. The store was stocked with wall-to-wall candy, everything from gummy bears and Gobstoppers to chocolate, taffy, and Twizzlers arranged in floor-to-ceiling glass containers. Just inside the entrance was a giant, flowing choco-late fountain with marshmallows and pretzels for dipping, and downstairs was a do-it-yourself ice-cream bar. The guests—both kids and grown-ups—could barely contain their excitement.

Mickey had carefully chosen her outfit for the day: a black satin trench coat with a red sweater, a plaid skirt, and a vintage heart-print scarf. She "disguised" herself in a pair of tortoiseshell glasses, hoping she'd blend in with the rest of the media covering the long red carpet outside.

"Heidi, over here!" one paparazzo shouted as Heidi Klum escorted her daughter Lou into the party. She obliged with a pose and a bright smile.

Normally, Mickey would have been starstruck by all the fashion celebs on the scene. But today she was looking for only one person: Cordy.

Victoria's limo pulled up and she stepped out of the car, holding Cordy's hand tightly.

The little girl looked miserable! She was wearing a white lace dress buttoned up to her neck, a white satin headband, frilly ankle socks, and shiny white Mary Janes. She noticed that Cordy's favorite pink pearls were wrapped around her wrist. Everything else she was wearing had been dictated and decided for her.

Oh no! Mickey thought. *That's not at all what she wanted to wear for her big day.* Her heart sank, knowing Jade had designed this prim-and-proper outfit for the little girl. But it was Cordy's birthday, and she should have been allowed to wear whatever she wanted.

As Victoria posed and paused at each reporter's

microphone to be interviewed, Mickey managed to push through the crowd and position herself in front of Cordy.

"Cordy!" Mickey shouted. "Over here!"

The little girl squinted at her. "Mickey? Is that you? Those are silly glasses!"

"Can I come to your party?"

Cordy made sure her granny was busy and motioned for Mickey to duck under the velvet rope and follow her. "This way," she said. "Let's play hide-and-seek with Granny Vicky."

While Victoria was giving interviews, Cordy silently slipped away and took Mickey's hand. The pair snuck into Dolly's through the back service-entrance door. Amazingly, no one noticed them in all the commotion outside. They hid behind a giant twenty-foot-tall chocolate teddy bear in the basement.

"How do you do that?" Mickey marveled.

"Do what?" Cordy asked, tugging at the neck of her dress.

"Disappear?"

Cordy shrugged. "Dunno. Granny Vicky says I'm the Cheshire Cat from Alice in Wonderland."

Mickey ruffled her curls. "You are! And I think I have a better idea for a game. Hide-and-seek isn't your granny's fave. This game is called 'Fashion Star.'"

Cordy's eyes lit up. "Ooh, fun! What do we do?"

"We figure out a way to make your party dress more Cordy, less icky," Mickey said.

"Yes! Yes!" Cordy cheered. "It's icky *and* itchy."

Mickey pulled a small sewing kit and fabric paints out of her tote bag.

"You design the skirt, and I'll loosen up the neckline and sleeves," she instructed the little girl.

Cordy stared at the paint markers. "It's okay to draw on my dress?" she asked.

"It's more than okay," Mickey assured her. "Make it your very own Cordy one-of-a-kind creation."

"But Granny and my nanny always tell me not to break stuff—or be loud or make a mess."

Mickey put an arm around her. "That's all very good advice, especially since you're a big girl now. Five is very grown up, you know."

Cordy considered. "It is?"

"Yes, but just because you have to follow the rules doesn't mean you can't make a few of your own. I listen to my mom and my teachers and my aunt Olive because they know what's best for me every day. But when it comes to my style, it's all me. I march to my own drummer. Fashion design is a great way to be yourself."

"Granny said I can't have drums. I asked for my fourth birthday. They give her a headache."

"Not real drums, Cordy," Mickey said, smiling.

"Imaginary ones. It means you hear your own music and you dance to it."

She took out her phone and searched for her favorite song, Taylor Swift's "Shake It Off." "I love to listen to this while I'm sewing," she told Cordy. "It makes me feel strong and invincible."

"What does that mean?" Cordy asked.

Mickey handed her a bright-pink paint marker and cranked up the song. "It means this dress is yours. Make it fancy and fabulous!"

By the time they had finished redesigning Cordy's outfit and slipped into the party room, Victoria was frantic. Cordy had been missing for nearly twenty minutes. The entire room was filled with heart-shaped balloons and pink streamers, and Cordy couldn't wait to get her hands on the three-tiered red velvet cake towering in the corner.

"Let's surprise her." Mickey held Cordy back. "Let's make a grand entrance." They ducked behind a giant gumball machine and waited for the perfect moment to jump out.

"You must find my granddaughter," Mickey overheard Victoria telling two security guards. "She's about three feet tall, with blond curls and dimples."

"Does she run away often?" one of the guards asked.

"Oh yes," Victoria replied. "All the time. You

take your eyes off her for a second and she's gone. I can't keep up, and since her mother left to pursue an acting career in California, I'm solely responsible for her."

"I see," said the other guard, taking notes. "She's a sly one."

"Yes, so smart and so full of energy," Victoria said. "She doesn't mean to be mischievous. She just can't help it. This is all my fault!"

Jade was standing at her side, trying to keep her calm. "I'm sure she just went off to play with some friends," she said. "I just hope she doesn't ruin my dress. It's very expensive Chantilly lace."

"Not to worry, we've locked down all the doors

in the candy store. She can't go far," the first guard said.

Mickey waited till the guards had gone off to search. "Okay, that's our cue, Cordy," she said, giving the little girl a gentle push. "Go show Granny Vicky how beautiful you are."

Cordy burst out from behind the gumball machine. "Ta-da!" she sang. Her entire dress was now covered in rainbow swirls and polka dots, and the sleeves and hem were frayed so they floated around her in a frenzy of fringe. The once buttoned-up collar was now a more comfy boat neck. And to accessorize, Mickey had drawn bunnies carrying balloons on Cordy's white Mary Janes.

"My dress!" Jade screamed. "You ruined it! You shredded it! It looks like a chopped salad!"

"I love it!" Cordy stood up to her. "It's my design, and it's my birthday, not yours. So there!" She stamped her foot.

Jade backed away as Victoria scooped her granddaughter into a big bear hug.

"Cordy, darling," Victoria exclaimed. "You scared Granny terribly. You could have been lost or hurt!"

"Nuh-uh, Granny," Cordy insisted. "I was with Mickey. She took good care of me, and she taught me to play my own drums."

Mickey stepped out from behind the gumball machine and blushed. "We had fun," she said.

"I should have known you were responsible for this," Jade suddenly piped up. She was furious. "You trashed my design."

"I didn't trash it," Mickey insisted. "I gave the client what she wanted. You never even thought to ask Cordy her opinion."

"I love my dress now," Cordy said, twirling around in it. "Isn't it beautiful, Granny?"

Victoria looked it over from top to bottom. "It's, it's…"

"Very Cordy," Mickey interrupted. "It's everything she is and wanted in a party dress. I just helped her bring her vision to life."

"I was going to say it's divine," Victoria added.

"Very unique, just like my Cordy. How do I thank you?"

"Um, maybe you could just send Mr. Kaye an email and tell him I fixed the problem from the WDAA luncheon?" Mickey said.

"I'll do more than that," Victoria vowed. "I'll tell him myself in person."

Class Act

When Mickey returned to Apparel Arts on Monday morning, she was surprised to find Victoria sitting at the front of the studio with Mr. Kaye.

"Why, that's very generous of you," he was telling the designer as Mickey took her seat.

"What's going on?" Gabriel whispered. "Why is that uppity lady here?"

"Get a clue!" South leaned forward and

smacked him on the head. "That uppity lady is Victoria Vanderweil."

"No way!" Gabriel whistled through his teeth. "Cool."

Mickey was afraid to guess the reason for Victoria's visit to FAB, but she hoped it wasn't to report to her teacher that she had crashed Cordy's party.

"Class," Mr. Kaye addressed the room, tapping a ruler on his desk. "Attention, please. I am happy to share some very exciting news with you all."

Mickey held her breath. It didn't sound like Victoria was ratting her out.

"Ms. Vanderweil wishes to commend FAB

and specifically one of our pupils for teaching her granddaughter a lesson in personal expression."

Mars elbowed Mickey. "It's you, isn't it?"

Mickey shrugged. She hoped so, but Mr. Kaye wasn't looking in her direction.

"We've all been invited to view the Victoria Vanderweil fall-winter collection on the runway during New York Fashion Week," Mr. Kaye continued. "It's a thrilling, once-in-a-lifetime opportunity for all of you…"

He turned to face Mickey. "And we have Mickey to thank for it."

The class cheered and Mickey felt her cheeks flush.

"My granddaughter has told me she wishes to follow in my footsteps," Victoria said to Mickey. "Considering last week she wanted to be an astronaut ballerina on the moon, it's a great improvement. She can't stop designing and redesigning all her clothes. She didn't run away all weekend because she was so busy! I'm very grateful, and I owe that to you."

Mickey smiled. "She always had it in her," she told Victoria. "I just believed in her."

"I assume you have someone who believes in you in the same way?" Victoria asked her.

"Lots of someones," Mickey said. "Mr. Kaye, JC, my mom, my aunt Olive."

"Then you are very lucky—and very talented," Victoria added, winking. "Why don't you bring all those someones along to my show. I'll make sure you have seats in the front row."

Aunt Olive and Mickey's mom had never been to a real New York Fashion Week show before. The excitement in the air was electric as everyone filed through the doors of the enormous Lincoln Center tent. Inside were rows and rows of seats for invited guests, and the press and their cameras were set up behind them to capture every moment.

"And I thought the runway was big at FAB," Mickey's mom, Jordana, said. "It's a mile long. Those poor models!"

"They're used to it," Mickey assured them. "Wait till you see the high heels they have to walk in."

JC and Mr. Kaye were already in their seats and waved from across the floor.

Mickey led her family to where they were seated and noticed that a group of front-row seats were labeled with her name on them. They read "Reserved for Mickey Williams, Kenzie Wills Designs."

"I feel like a celeb!" she exclaimed, sitting down next to JC.

"Not so fast," JC said, pointing to the group of seats next to them. "Check out who's sitting with us." Mickey looked at the paper taped to the chair that read "Kim Kardashian."

"I'm going to faint," Mickey said, fanning herself with the program.

"Not if I beat you to it," JC insisted. A yelp from inside his bag seconded that.

"You brought Madonna?" Mickey whispered. "To New York Fashion Week?"

"Hey, where I go, she goes," JC insisted. "Besides, Madonna is a celebrity in her own right. Isn't that so, pup?" The Chihuahua yapped back approvingly.

Mickey scanned the tent as the seats began to fill up. "Have you seen Cordy?" she asked.

"Nope. So far, so good," JC reported. "Not a food fight, blackout, or fashion catastrophe in sight. I think you really got through to her."

Mickey noticed Mars, South, Gabriel, and the rest of her Apparel Arts classmates a few rows behind them. She waved.

"Wasn't it supposed to start at four o'clock?" Olive asked Mr. Kaye. "These fashion people aren't very punctual, are they?"

"You know the expression 'fashionably late'?" he asked her. "Well, that certainly applies to the runway."

But Mickey didn't mind. She could have sat there all day and night and just absorbed the buzz. Being in this tent gave her such a rush. This was where she belonged, where she always dreamed she would be. Today, she was in the audience. But one day, she would be up there on that runway, sending her models to strut down it wearing her own designs. She knew it. She felt it in every bone in her body.

Her mom read her mind and squeezed her hand. "One day, this will be your show, Mickey Mouse," she said. "I believe in you."

Suddenly, the lights dimmed.

"It's about time!" Olive sniffed. She took a

container of kale juice out of her bag and offered it to Mr. Kaye.

"Don't mind if I do," he said.

A hush fell over the room as Victoria walked out onto the stage to welcome her guests. "This collection was inspired by my love for my granddaughter," she told the audience. "It's called 'Youthful Exuberance,' and I hope you enjoy it."

On with the Show

As the music began pumping through the speakers, a cloud of pink fog rolled onto the stage.

"Whoa, this is awesome," JC said, perching himself on the edge of his seat.

The first model came strutting out, dressed in a pale-pink velvet kimono wrap dress. Her eyeshadow and lipstick were both silver, and she looked like she had fairy dust in her long, wild curls.

"Very ethereal," Mr. Kaye whispered to Olive. "Don't you agree?"

"It reminds me of one of the fairies in Shakespeare's *A Midsummer Night's Dream*," Olive whispered.

Mr. Kaye nodded, impressed. "A very keen observation!"

Next up was a pantsuit look: white trousers with a white tuxedo jacket. The model was wearing pigtails tied with long, white chiffon ribbons flowing down her back.

"Exquisite," Mr. Kaye gushed.

"Won't it get dirty easily?" Olive asked.

"Head-to-toe white is a huge trend right now—but you have a valid point."

One by one, the looks came down the runway: a pink tutu minidress with a houndstooth blazer and black ankle boots; a pale-lavender column gown with vibrant purple satin elbow-length gloves.

"Now those gloves I like," Olive said. "They'd go well with my jacket."

Mickey's favorite look by far was a dove-gray ball gown with delicate beading at the bodice and miles of ruffled tiers. It floated down the runway, and the color was very gentle and unexpected: a modern twist on a traditional "princessy" gown.

As Victoria came out at the end of the show, the crowd rose to their feet and applauded wildly.

Walking at her side was Cordy—and she was wearing the dress Mickey had made for her!

"Are you seeing what I'm seeing?" JC almost fell out of his chair. "Mick, that's your dress on the runway at New York Fashion Week!"

Mickey could hardly believe her eyes, and she didn't know what to do when Cordy suddenly jumped off the stage and grabbed her from the audience.

"Come!" she insisted, dragging her back up with her. There Mickey stood, holding Cordy's hand on one side and Victoria's on the other as they bowed together.

"That's my girl!" Olive sobbed. Mr. Kaye

offered her his handkerchief, and she blew her nose in it loudly.

Mickey's mom stood up on her chair and whistled through her teeth. "Go, Mickey!" she yelled, and Mickey's classmates all joined in.

Mickey hoped her enthusiastic friends and family wouldn't upset Victoria. It was, after all, her show. Instead, the designer insisted she step forward with Cordy and take her own bow.

"Please give a hand for the real Youthful Exuberance," Victoria said, pointing to them.

Mickey had never felt so proud and so alive.

⋆ Back to the Drawing Board ⋆

When Mr. Kaye walked in the classroom the next day, it was business as usual. "Take out your sketchbooks," he said, not even pausing to drop his jacket or bag on his chair.

He grabbed a marker and wrote a number six on the SMART Board. "Toughest assignment of the year," he warned them. "I hope you'll all ready."

South raised her hand. "Tougher than No Sew

and Cordy Vanderweil's party dress? I doubt it," she said.

"That was child's play," Mr. Kaye insisted. "You've all experienced New York Fashion Week, so it's time to step up your game."

He tapped a key on the board, and a slide of one of Victoria's collection appeared on the screen.

"You'll be playing fashion critic," he said. "I want your opinion on what you saw—what was good, what was bad, what you would change. A thousand-word report on my desk by Friday."

"You want us to critique Victoria Vanderweil's fall-winter collection?" Gabriel gasped. "And one thousand words? Does 'a' count as a word?"

"If there are nine hundred ninety-nine other words beside it," Mr. Kaye said. "And this assignment comes from Victoria herself. She wants to read every single one of your reports."

Gabriel banged his head on his desk. "This just keeps getting worse!"

Mr. Kaye flipped through the slides. "Choose three you want to critique, and one that you would like to reinvent. Use it to inspire your own personal design."

"What's the budget?" Mars asked.

"As usual, twenty dollars and feel free to choose scraps from the fabric bin."

"Are there any guidelines?" South asked.

"For once, there are none," Mr. Kaye said. "Use your imagination and make it your own." He flipped to a picture of Cordy and Mickey taking a bow. "The sky's the limit."

But Mickey didn't even notice he was showing her picture to the class. She was already buried in her sketchbook, dreaming up her next design.

Carrie's Style File:
Meet Project Runway Winner
Michelle Lesniak

Obviously, I am a HUGE *Project Runway* fan—and season eleven's winner, Michelle Lesniak, is one of my fave designers. She recently rocked the runway on *Project Runway All Stars*, making it all the way to the final four. Her clothes have an effortlessly cool vibe to them, and I love how they move. Michelle was nice enough to answer all my questions. Check out her line at michellelesniak.com!

Carrie: When did you know you were going to be a designer?

Michelle: I've always designed. I don't think it's about it becoming your career; it's part of who you are. Even if I don't design to pay my bills, I'll always be a designer!

Carrie: Who taught you to sew and how old were you?

Michelle: My mother and grandmother taught me to sew. I probably picked up my first needle when I was five or six.

Carrie: What is the best part of being a fashion designer? What is the hardest part?

Michelle: I don't know if it's necessarily being a designer, but any career you do out of love is really great. Whether it's designing clothing, being an interior designer, or being a chef: following your dreams and doing what you love to do is the best part.

The hardest part about being a fashion designer is that it's a tough industry. Getting people to realize the value of a garment in this day of throwaway fashion is really difficult. It can be challenging to pay your bills.

Carrie: How would you describe your design aesthetic?

Michelle: Emotional, layered, romantic, fairy tale–like, whimsical in some aspects, sometimes a little dark.

Carrie: What designers do you idolize?

Michelle: Designers that can bounce back from financial failure or troubles. Jil Sander is one. Designers that can transform the marketplace: Bottega Veneta. And designers who wear their hearts on their sleeves.

Carrie: What was it like being on *Project Runway* twice? And *winning*?

Michelle: It was incredibly difficult both times, but not an experience I would trade in for the world. I've met some of the closest friends I've ever had as well as really honed my designs and aesthetic.

Carrie: What advice do you have for kids who want to grow up and follow in your footsteps?

Michelle: There are so many different careers in the fashion industry. Don't become frustrated if you're not good at drawing or sewing, because you can still find a career even though you may have weaknesses in some areas.

Acknowledgments

Many thanks to all our friends and family: Daddy, Maddie, The Kahns, Berks, and Saps: love you to the moon and back!

A big thanks to the inspiring Michelle Lesniak of *Project Runway* for her interview. Mickey wishes she can be you when she grows up!

To all our great friends at Vital Theatre for the AMAZING musical adaptation of *Fashion Academy*—thank you all for bringing the characters to life. Steve, Sam, Jaimie, Kyle, Julz, Michael, Shani, Annjolyn…couldn't have asked for a better team. To our brilliant cast, you brought such joy to the stage with your talent and heart. Thank you, thank you, thank you, and bravo!

And last but not least, a ginormous thank-you and shout-out to the gifted Sabrina Chap for the endless hours, endless laughs, and your brilliant music, lyrics, and partnership on the script.

Girl, you rocked it!

To Katherine Latshaw at Folio—always our cheerleader; to the gang at Sourcebooks: Steve, Kate, Alex, Elizabeth. We are so happy and proud to be with you!

"Ooh, la la!" JC exclaimed as Mickey walked into the hallway of FAB wearing an Eiffel Tower print T-shirt, a can-can inspired tiered ruffle skirt, and a purple studded beret.

"You like?" she said, giving her ensemble a twirl. She'd paired it with a mismatched pair of combat boots—one purple, one pink.

"It's certainly very Parisian," JC said. "All you need is a croissant-shaped purse to go with it."

Mickey pulled a long gold tube-shaped bag out of her backpack. "Baguette," she said. "I'm one step ahead of you."

"So what's with all the French-ness?" her friend asked.

"Didn't you hear about the international student runway competition?" she replied. "Mr. Stitchman insists someone from FAB win—or else."

JC raised an eyebrow. "Win what?"

Mickey closed her eyes and sighed. "Only a trip to Paris Fashion Week—and the opportunity to present your designs at a FIFI gala."

"FIFI?" JC gasped. "As in the French Institute of Fashion Industries?"

Mickey nodded. "Amazing right?"

"Amazing—and near to impossible. Every fashion student in the world is probably competing."

"I know," Mickey said. "Which is why I need your help. I've never been anywhere out of the country, and I don't know anything about Paris—except for what I'm wearing. Oh, and those colorful little sandwich cookies."

"Macarons," JC corrected her. "I have visited Laudere in France several times…"

"You did mention that…several times," Mickey chuckled. "Something about staying with your cousin Angelique? Eating crepes and shopping on the Champs-Élysées?"

JC nodded. "My cuz moved to France a few years ago. She's very cool—and very fashionable."

Mickey sighed. "Do I have to beg?"

JC's Chihuahua Madonna made a whimpering noise from inside her dog bag.

"Can you top that?" JC snickered.

"JC…"

"Fine. No begging necessary."

"There's just one little thing, before you agree," Mickey added.

JC raised his hand to silence her. "Don't tell me. Does it wear a tiara and a bad attitude?"

Mickey nodded. "Jade is determined to win. She and Jake are partnering up as usual."

"And you think I'm afraid of the tantrum twins?" JC asked. "Pullease. You shouldn't be either. You can't cover up boring with bling. And you…well, you're one of a kind, Mick."

Mickey blushed. "You really think so? How many times has Jade beat me on fashion challenges? And how many times has she gotten us in trouble with Mr. Stitchman?"

"Too many. Which means she's running out of options. Besides, I bet you've already been working up ideas while Jade was out getting her mani and pedi."

"Well, I was thinking of doing a mini collection that draws from the iconic architecture of Paris. The Eiffel Tower, the Arch de Triomphe…"

"Love!" JC cheered. "Tell me more!"

Mickey pulled her sketchbook out of her bag. "Maybe colors that are muted, like grays and blues and charcoal to match the structures. Metallic silver and bronze, studding that looks like rivets. And the shape of this skirt—"

She showed him a dramatic A-line gown with a corseted back. "This mimics the lines of the tower."

"It's amazing," JC said breathlessly. "C'est magnifique."

"Is that good?" Mickey asked. "I don't speak any French."

"Oui! Oui!" JC added. "Translation: we've got this!"

"So it's a yes?" Mickey asked.

JC smiled slyly. "Madonna? What do you say to joining Team Mickey?"

Madonna yapped happily.

"That's a yes for both of us," JC said. "Paris Fashion Week, here we come."

About the Authors

Sheryl Berk has written about fashion for more than twenty years, first as a contributor to *InStyle* magazine and later as the founding editor in chief of *Life & Style Weekly*. She has written dozens of books with celebrities including Britney Spears, Jenna Ushkowitz, Whitney Port, and Zendaya—and the #1 *New*

York Times bestseller (turned movie) *Soul Surfer* with Bethany Hamilton. Her daughter, Carrie Berk, is a renowned cupcake connoisseur and blogger (www.facebook.com/PLCCupcakeClub; https://carriescupcakecritique.shutterfly.com) with more than 101,000 followers at the tender age of twelve! Carrie is a fountain of fabulous ideas for book series—she came up with Fashion Academy in the fifth grade. Carrie learned to sew from her grandma "Gaga" and has outfitted many an American Girl doll in original fashions. The Berks also write the deliciously popular series The Cupcake Club.

Check out Carrie's new fashion blog:

fashionacademybook.com and Instagram:

@fashionacademybook.